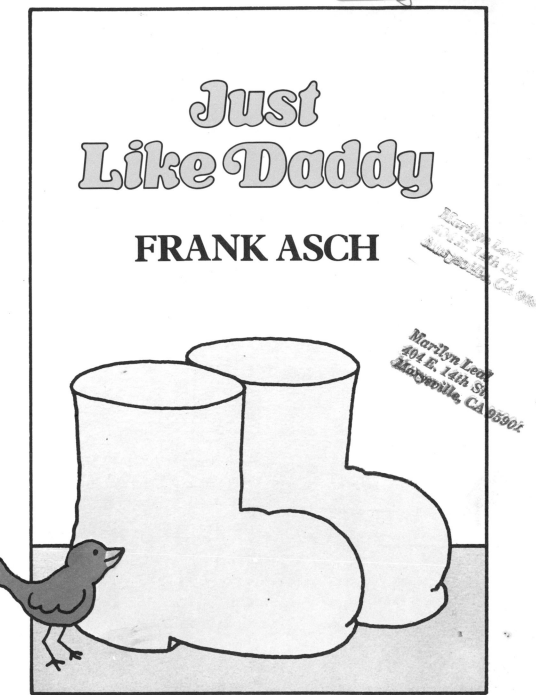

Just Like Daddy

FRANK ASCH

Prentice-Hall Books for Young Readers
A Division of Simon & Schuster, Inc., New York

Copyright ©1981 by Frank Asch
All rights reserved
including the right of reproduction
in whole or in part in any form.
Published by Prentice-Hall Books for Young Readers
A Division of Simon & Schuster, Inc.
Simon & Schuster Building
Rockefeller Center
1230 Avenue of the Americas
New York, NY 10020

10 9 8 7 6 5 4

10 9 8 7 6 5 4 3   pbk

Prentice-Hall Books for Young Readers
is a trademark of Simon & Schuster, Inc.
Manufactured in the United States of America

Library of Congress in Publication Data
Asch, Frank.   Just like Daddy.
SUMMARY: A very young bear describes all the activities
he does during the day that are just like his daddy's.
[1. Fathers—Fiction. 2. Bears—Fiction.]
I. Title.   PZ7.A778Ju
[E]   80-26000   ISBN 0-13-514042-0
ISBN 0-13-514035-8 pbk

To Devin

When I got up this morning
I yawned a big yawn…

Just like Daddy.

I washed my face, got dressed,
and had a big breakfast…

Just like Daddy.

Then I put on my coat
and my boots…

Just like Daddy.

And we all went fishing.

On the way I picked a flower
and gave it to my mother…

Just like Daddy.

When we got to the lake,
I put a big worm on my hook…

Just like Daddy.

All day we fished and fished,
and I caught a big fish…

Just like Mommy!